Little Red Riding Hood

Adapted from

The Brothers Grimm

by

Gennady Spirin

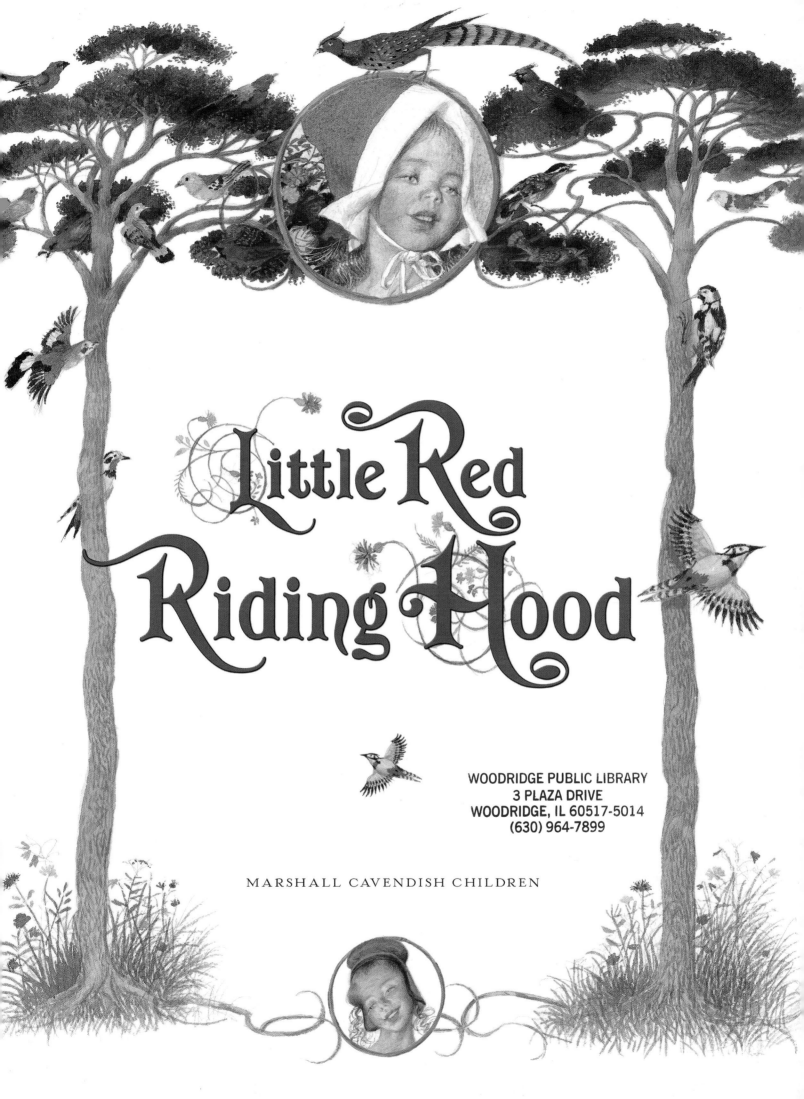

Little Red Riding Hood

MARSHALL CAVENDISH CHILDREN

A NOTE ABOUT THE STORY

The tale, "Little Red Riding Hood," has appeared in many versions throughout history. As far back as the fourteenth century, a French oral variant depicted the wolf as a werewolf and Little Red Riding Hood as a smart little girl who escapes the wolf's advances by using her wits. In 1697, the French writer Charles Perrault published a version, "*Le Petit Chaperon Rouge,*" in *Histoires ou contes du temps passé, avec des moralités (Stories or Tales of Past Times with Morals)*, in which he introduced the red hood and described Little Red Riding Hood as an "attractive, well-bred young lady" who later gets eaten by the wolf.

My retelling is based on the Brothers Grimm's earliest version, *Rotkäppchen,* published in 1812 in *Kinder-und Hausmärchen (Children's and Household Tales)*, but, as in the Russian story that I heard as a child, I included two hunters instead of one. I omitted also the scene in which Little Red Riding Hood and her grandmother place stones in the wolf's stomach before he dies.

I enjoyed illustrating and retelling the version you find here, as "Little Red Riding Hood" has always been one of my favorite tales.

—Gennady Spirin

Text and illustrations copyright © 2010 by Gennady Spirin • All rights reserved • Marshall Cavendish Corporation, 99 White Plains Road, Tarrytown, NY 10591 • www.marshallcavendish.us/kids

LIBRARY OF CONGRESS CATALOGING-IN-PUBLICATION DATA
Spirin, Gennady. Little Red Riding Hood / adapted from The Brothers Grimm by Gennady Spirin. — 1st ed. p. cm. Summary: A little girl meets a hungry wolf in the forest while on her way to visit her grandmother. Includes a note about the history of the tale. ISBN 978-0-7614-5704-6 [1. Fairy tales. s2. Folklore—Germany.] I. Grimm, Wilhelm, 1786-1859. II. Grimm, Jacob, 1785-1863. III. Little Red Riding Hood. English. IV. Title. PZ8.1.S76733Li 2010 398.20943'02—dc22 2009046643

The illustrations are rendered in watercolor and colored pencil.
Book design by Michael Nelson   Editor: Margery Cuyler
Printed in Malaysia (T)   First edition
3 5 6 4 2

mc Marshall Cavendish
Children

For my grandson, Nikolai

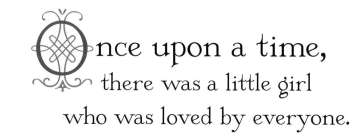

Once upon a time,
there was a little girl
who was loved by everyone.

She wore a red hood that was a gift from her grandmother. The little girl liked it so much that she never took it off, and that's why she became known as Little Red Riding Hood.

One day, Little Red Riding Hood's mother said to her, "Would you take this cake to your grandmother? She is sick in bed, and this food will make her feel better. Mind your manners and do not leave the path for any reason."

Little Red Riding Hood
took the basket and set off.
As she was walking through the woods,
she met a large wolf.

"Good morning," said the wolf. "Where are
you going so early in the day?"

"To Grandmother's house," said Little Red
Riding Hood. "She's sick in bed, and my
mother says the cake in this basket will make
her feel better."

"Oh," said the wolf. "And where does your
grandmother live?"

"She lives in a house under three big oak
trees," said Little Red Riding Hood.

"I know just where that
is," said the wolf.

The wolf walked along with
Little Red Riding Hood for a
while. Then he said, "Why don't
you stop and pick some flowers?"

"I'll pick a bouquet for my
grandmother," said Little Red
Riding Hood.

So she left the path to pick
some flowers while the wolf said
good-bye and ran straight to her
grandmother's house.

He knocked on the door.

TAP! TAP! TAP!

"Who's there?" came an old, crackly voice.

"Little Red Riding Hood," said the wolf in a voice as sweet as honey.

"Come right in," said Grandmother. "I'm sick in bed."

The wolf opened the door and saw the grandmother lying against a big pillow.

Before she could even blink, the wolf jumped
on her bed and gobbled her up!

Then he put on one of her bed caps and pulled the covers up to his neck.

Soon, along came Little Red Riding Hood.

She knocked on the door.

TAP! TAP! TAP!

"Who's there?" asked the wicked wolf in an old woman's voice.

"It's Little Red Riding Hood, and I've brought you some cake from Mother."

"Come in," called the wolf.

Little Red Riding Hood
opened the door, walked over
to her grandmother's bed, and
climbed up.

"Oh, Grandmother, what
big hands you have!" said
Little Red Riding Hood.

"The better to hug you
with," said the wicked wolf.

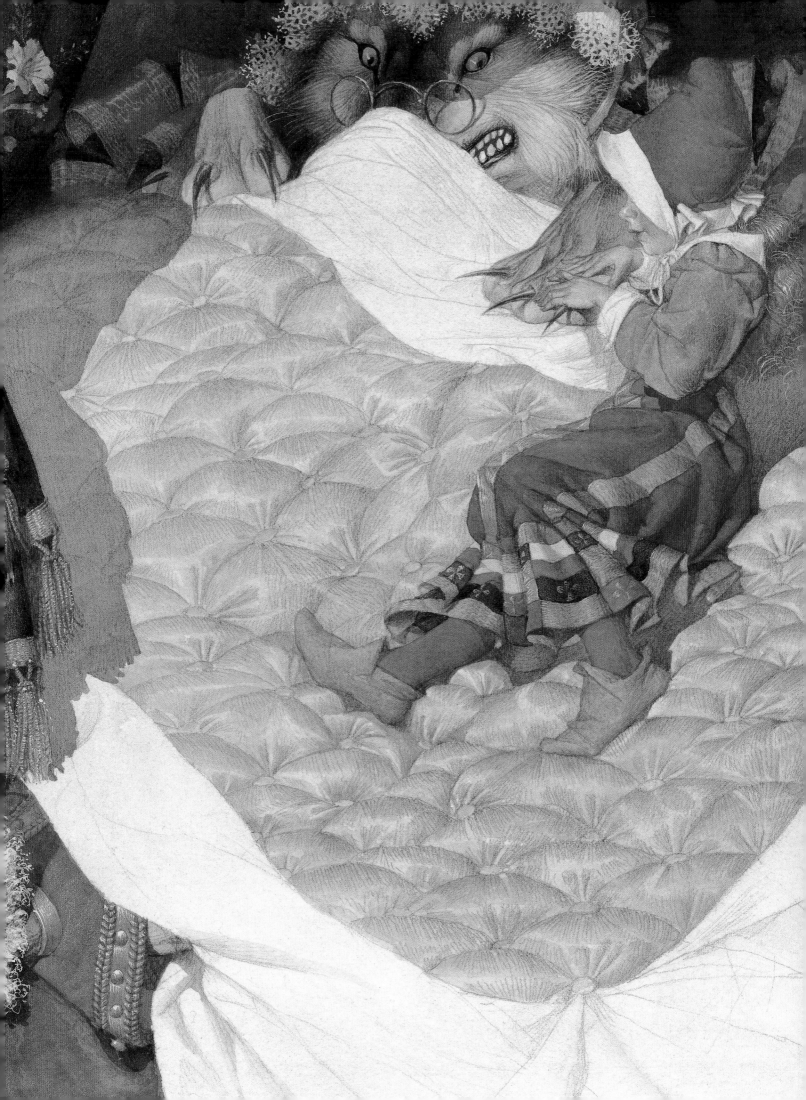

"Oh, Grandmother, what big ears you have," said Little Red Riding Hood.

"The better to hear you with," said the wicked wolf.

"Oh, Grandmother, what big eyes you have," said Little Red Riding Hood.

"The better to see you with," said the wicked wolf.

"Oh, Grandmother, what big teeth you have," said Little Red Riding Hood.

"The better to eat you with!" said the wicked wolf.

And with that, he leaped out of bed and swallowed Little Red Riding Hood in one, big gulp. Then he climbed back under the covers and fell fast asleep. Soon he was snoring.

After a while, two hunters passed by the house.

"How the old lady snores," said one. "Let's see if she is all right."

They pushed open the door and saw the wolf lying in the grandmother's bed.

"A great big wolf!" shouted the hunters. The wolf woke up and jumped to the floor.

The hunters lifted their guns to shoot him, but then they noticed the wolf's fat stomach.

"I bet that wicked wolf ate the old woman!" they yelled.

"Let's open up his stomach and see!"

They chased the wolf outdoors, took one of
their hunting knives, and cut open his stomach.

Out jumped Little Red Riding Hood and her
grandmother!

"It was dark in there!" cried Little Red Riding
Hood. "I was so frightened!" She grabbed her
grandmother's hand, and they ran back into the
house as fast as they could go.

"I feel so much better," said Grandmother as she sat down in her favorite chair. Then she ate the cake that her granddaughter had brought her.

Little Red Riding Hood climbed into her grandmother's lap. "I will never leave the path again when my mother tells me not to," she said, and she gave her grandmother a hug and a kiss.